Apr. 16, 2007

A Beginning-to-Read Book

The Cookie House

by Margaret Hillert

Illustrated by Kinuko Craft

Get up. Get up.
Come with us.
We will go to work.

Oh, this is fun.
We can run and jump.
We like it here.

You two play here.
You do not have to work.
We will go now.
But we will come back to get you.

Look here.
Here is something for us.
Something we like.
Have one.

And here is something.
It is little.
It can play with us.

Mother is not here.
Father is not here.
I do not like this.

We can not find the way.
What can we do now?
Who will help us?
I want to go.

We can not go now.
Come down here with me.
Come down, down, down.

Get up. Get up.
Look what I see.
Can you see it, too?
Look up, up.

Look at it go.
We can go, too.
Run, run, run.

Oh, see the little house.
I like it.
I like it.
What fun for us.

Look at this and this and this.
I want one.
You can have one, too.

No, you can not.
You can not have that.
It is not for you.

Oh, help, help.
I do not like it in here.
Help me.
Help me.

Here I come.
I will help you.
See me help.

Go in. Go in.
We do not like you.
I will make you go in.
In you go.

Come away.
Come away.

Here we go.
Run, run, run.

What is this?
What can we do now?
We can not go in here.

Oh, look at us.
What fun.
What a ride this is!

I see Father.
Father, Father.
Here we are, Father.

The following activities support the findings of the National Reading Panel that determined the most effective components for reading instruction are: Phonemic Awareness, Phonics, Vocabulary, Fluency, and Text Comprehension.

Phonemic Awareness: The /k/ sound

Oddity Task: Say the /**k**/ sound for your child. Ask your child to say the word that has the /**k**/ sound in the following word groups:

kid, rid, bid	rot, run, rock	pan, pat, pack
dot, Don, dock	Sam, sat, sack	rind, kind, mind

Phonics: The letter Kk

1. Demonstrate how to form the letters **K** and **k** for your child.
2. Have your child practice writing **K** and **k** at least three times each.
3. Write down the following words and ask your child to circle the letter **k** in each word:

back	kit	make	king	rocket
look	work	like	lock	kitten
bucket	truck	key	milk	chicken

Vocabulary: Nouns and Verbs

1. Write the following words on separate pieces of paper and point to them as you read them to your child:

go	mother	house	jump	father
boy	work	run	girl	tree

2. Point to each word and read it aloud to your child. Ask your child to repeat the word.

3. Explain to your child that words describing people, places, and things are called nouns and that words describing actions are called verbs.

4. Divide a piece of paper in half vertically and write the words nouns and verbs at the top, one word in each column.

5. Ask your child to sort the words on the pieces of paper by placing them in the correct column depending on whether the word on the paper is a noun or a verb.

6. Continue identifying nouns and verbs by playing a game in which one of you names a noun and the other names a verb to go with the noun (for example; dog/bark, baby/cry, grass/grow, flower/bloom, car/drive, etc.)

Fluency: Echo Reading

1. Reread the story to your child at least two more times while your child tracks the print by running a finger under the words as they are read. Ask your child to read the words he or she knows with you.

2. Reread the story, stopping after each sentence or page to allow your child to read (echo) what you have read. Repeat echo reading and let your child take the lead.

Text Comprehension: Discussion Time

1. Ask your child to retell the sequence of events in the story.

2. To check comprehension, ask your child the following questions:

   • What happened to the children when the mother and father left to work?

   • How do you think the boy and girl felt when they got lost?

   • Do you think it was a good idea for the boy and girl to follow the bird? Why or why not?

   • Would you have eaten the cookies on the house? Why or why not?

   • What lesson do you think the boy and girl learned?

WORD LIST

The Cookie House **uses the 59 words listed below.**

This list can be used to practice reading the words that appear in the text. You may wish to write the words on index cards and use them to help your child build automatic word recognition. Regular practice with these words will enhance your child's fluency in reading connected text.

a	get	make	that
and	go	me	the
are		mother	this
at	have		to
away	help	no	too
	here	not	two
back	house	now	
but			up
	I	oh	us
can	in	one	
come	is		want
	it	play	way
do		ride	we
down	jump	run	what
			who
father	like	see	will
find	little	something	with
for	look		work
fun			
			you

ABOUT THE AUTHOR   Margaret Hillert has written over 80 books for children who are just learning to read. Her books have been translated into many different languages and over a million children throughout the world have read her books. She first started writing poetry as a child and has continued to write for children and adults throughout her life. A first grade teacher for 34 years, Margaret is now retired from teaching and lives in Michigan where she likes to write, take walks in the morning, and care for her three cats.

Photograph by Glenna Washburn

ABOUT THE ADVISER   Shannon Cannon contributed the activities pages that appear in this book. Shannon serves as a literacy consultant and provides staff development to help improve reading instruction. She is a frequent presenter at educational conferences and workshops. Prior to this she worked as an elementary school teacher and as president of a curriculum publishing company.